A. Beasty Bites

B. Jungle Java

C. Savanna Library

D. House of Bones

E. Amazon Security

F. Everyday School

G. Wild 'n' Wooly
   Barber Shop

H. Arctic House
   Post Office

I. Monkey Bowl

J. Porpoise Pool

K. Big Cat Toys

L. Gator Grocery

Hayley

Harley

Pouch

Squirt

Mr. Turtellini

Boyd

Dedicated to children everywhere who love to read

—J. M.

To Mary Linda

—M.S.

ZONDERKIDZ

Wonderfully Made
Copyright © 2013 by Joyce Meyer
Illustrations © 2013 by Zondervan

Requests for information should be addressed to:

Zonderkidz, 5300 Patterson Ave SE, Grand Rapids, Michigan 49530

ISBN: 978-0-310-72353-0

Joyce Meyer is represented by Thomas J. Winters of Winters, King & Associates, Inc., Tulsa, Oklahoma.

Zonderkidz is a trademark of Zondervan.

Illustrator: Mary Sullivan
Contributors: Jill Gorey, Nancy Haller
Editor: Barbara Herndon
Art direction and design: Cindy Davis

Printed in China

13 14 15 /LPC/ 10 9 8 7 6 5 4 3 2 1

JOYCE MEYER

Wonderfully Made

pictures by **MARY SULLIVAN**

ZONDER**kidz**

ZONDERVAN.com/
AUTHOR**TRACKER**
follow your favorite authors

Hayley Hippo's heart skipped a beat as she looked at the flyer.

EVERYDAY
ZOO'S
First Annual
Talent Show

All around her, the zoo was bubbling with activity ... singing and
dancing and flapping and tap-tap-tapping. It seemed like everybody
was going to be in the talent show.

Even Mr. Turtellini, the zoo's oldest inhabitant, was planning on telling jokes.

More than anything, Hayley wanted to be in the show too, but she was having trouble finding the right talent.

First Book
for
French Horn

EVERYDAY ZOO BAKE-OFF!

Hayley

Arnold

"Hi, Hayley!" Gabby Goose shouted as she flew overhead. "What are *you* doing for the talent show?"

"I don't know," said Hayley, feeling a little discouraged.

"I'm either going to do some flying tricks or honk 'Ode to Joy,'" Gabby announced. "Would you like to be part of my act?"

Hayley shook her head. "No thanks. I don't fly or honk very well."

As Gabby flew off, Hayley let out a sigh. "Maybe God forgot to give me a talent."

"Nonsense!" barked the police chief. "God doesn't forget!"

"Sarge is right," Pouch chimed in. "God gives all of us unique gifts. We just have to discover what they are."

"Wow, I never knew there were so many different talents," Hayley said. "I guess all I have to do is find the right one for me!"

Everyday Zoo Talent Show!
Participants

Mr. Turtellini – stand-up comedy
Boyd – magician
Harley – magician's assistant
Gabby – flying/honking
Squirt – bouncing ball
y – acrobatics
imble – singing
· shadow puppets
Midge & Pidge – ice skat'

And off Hayley went to see what clever things her other friends were doing for the show.

Hayley's first stop was Porpoise Pool to visit Squirt the Seal. "Smile for the camera!" Hayley shouted as she photographed Squirt in action. Squirt was amazing! The things he could do with that ball!

He tossed it,

flipped it,

rolled it, zipped it.

"How do you like my act?" Squirt asked when his routine was finished.

"Don't you mean *our* act?" Arnold chimed in.

"You guys are fantastic!" Hayley told her friends. "Maybe I could do something like that for the show!"

But no matter how hard Hayley tried, her ball didn't flip, roll, or zip.

It just flew through the air and broke a lamp.

Next, Hayley stopped by to see Boyd and Harley. Their act was magical.

Boyd pulled a rabbit out of his hat,

turned his magic wand into a colorful flower,

and even made Harley disappear!

Hayley was so impressed she ran right home to try some magic tricks of her own.

Hayley flipped over Missy Monkey's awesome acrobatics.

Who would have guessed that Miss Bimble could sing?

And Sarge's shadow puppets were spectacular!

But none of these were Hayley's special talent.

The next day, Hayley visited Midge and Pidge.

"I love ice skating," Hayley told the twins.

"Then join us, dollface!" cried Pidge.

"Please, do!" encouraged Midge.

"But be careful," the worrywarts warned. "You could fall and hit your funny bone!" "Or freeze your bottom!" "Or get your tongue stuck on the ice!"

Hayley was certain this would be her special talent for the show. After all, she was a good skater. She could skate forwards and backwards and even do loop-de-loops.

Unfortunately, the one thing she couldn't do was stop.

"What's wrong with me?" Hayley cried. "I'm terrible at everything!"

The little hippo hung her head. "Why can't I be talented like everyone else?"

Pouch walked up and knelt down beside her. "Hayley, God didn't make you to be like everyone else. He made you to be *you*!"

"But my friends..." Hayley sniffled. "They're all so...AWESOME!"

"Yes, they are," said Pouch. "And that's exactly how God sees *you*! You are wonderfully made and perfect in his eyes."

"Perfect? But I can't do *anything* well!"

"Of course you can," said Midge.

"Don't you worry, honey pie," said Pidge. "You'll find your talent."

"Sometimes we're just not looking in the right place," said Pouch. Then, he added with a twinkle in his eye, "Who knows? Maybe your talent is right in front of your eyes!"

The night of the show finally arrived. The acts were hair-raising, heartfelt, and hilarious.

When it was time for the last act of the evening, Master of Ceremonies Pouch addressed the audience. "And now to close this wonderful show, please welcome the very talented … Hayley Hippo!"

It was so quiet you could hear a pin drop as all the animals looked at Hayley, wondering what she would do.

"I didn't think I had a talent," Hayley announced to the crowd, "but then my friends helped me discover something I'm actually good at." And with a nod to Pouch, the curtain opened...

The audience gave Hayley a standing ovation. The little hippo was grateful that God had not only blessed her with talent … but with some very good friends too.

I praise you because I am fearfully and wonderfully made.
Psalm 139:14